DISNEP
ENCHANTED
True Love's Kiss

Adapted by Sarah Nathan
Based on the screenplay written by Bill Kelly
Executive Producers Chris Chase, Sunil Perkash, Ezra Swerdlow
Produced by Barry Josephson and Barry Sonnenfeld
Directed by Kevin Lima

DISNEP PRESS
New York

Chapter 1

Deep in the forest, in a magical
kingdom known as Andalasia, there lived
a fair maiden. Her name was Giselle.
She was kind to animals and loved by all
who knew her. There was only one thing
missing in her life—true love's kiss.

Giselle's best friend was a chipmunk named Pip. Even though he was small, his heart was big. He liked to look after Giselle.

Then, one day, a large troll attacked Giselle. Pip tried to save her, but he couldn't do it alone.

Luckily, a handsome prince named Edward was riding by and helped save Giselle from the troll. As soon as Prince Edward and Giselle saw each other, they fell in love. "We shall be married in the morning!" the prince exclaimed.

Looking in her crystal ball, Edward's
stepmother, Queen Narissa, saw the
meeting. She was *not* happy. If Edward
and Giselle got married, Narissa
would no longer rule the kingdom.
She decided to send Giselle far away
from Andalasia.

The next morning was the royal wedding. Giselle's animal friends helped her make a beautiful white gown. Then she went to meet her prince. But on the way, an old lady stopped Giselle—and pushed her into a wishing well! Poor Giselle had been tricked by the evil Queen Narissa dressed as an old lady!

Giselle tumbled down a dark tunnel. Her arms and legs felt strange. With a thump, she landed in the dark. When she climbed outside, she realized that she was *very* far from Andalasia.

Chapter 2

This new land was not at all magical.
It was loud and dirty. People were not
very nice to Giselle. And no one
could tell her how to find the castle or
her prince.

But that was about to change. A
handsome man named Robert and his
daughter, Morgan, were on their way
home when they spotted Giselle. She
was high up on a billboard—and she
was slipping! Robert rushed over,
opened his arms, and caught her.

When she was safe, Giselle told Robert and Morgan about her prince and true love's kiss. "It's the most powerful thing in the world," she said. Robert was not so sure about that. But since it was raining and Giselle had nowhere to go, Robert and Morgan brought her to their home. After her long day, Giselle quickly fell asleep.

The next day, Robert brought Giselle to his office. Then they went for a walk in Central Park. "What is it with you and this prince of yours?" Robert asked.

Giselle told him they had fallen in love the moment they met. Robert explained that he and his girlfriend, Nancy, had been dating for five years.

That did not make sense to Giselle. "How does she know that you love her?" she asked in a singsong voice. Robert was embarrassed by her singing. But everybody else thought it was lovely. Street musicians picked up the melody and sang along with Giselle. Soon, even Robert was smiling.

Robert asked Giselle to dinner that night. At the restaurant, the waiter brought Giselle a pretty drink. This was no ordinary drink. It had been poisoned by someone working for Queen Narissa. Luckily, Giselle did not take a sip!

The next morning, Prince Edward
arrived. He had come all the way from
Andalasia to find Giselle. She was very
happy to see him. But saying good-bye
to Robert and Morgan was harder than
Giselle could have imagined.

Chapter 3

Giselle did not want to go back to
Andalasia right away. She wanted
to go on a date with Edward. While
they were on their date, Giselle asked
her prince if he wanted to go to a
costume ball that evening. He agreed!

With no fairy godmother in sight,
Giselle was worried. How would she
get ready for the ball? Luckily, Morgan
came to the rescue.

She knew the right stores to go
to and all the accessories a princess
would need for a ball! Soon, Giselle
was ready.

When they arrived at the ball, Giselle
and Prince Edward looked around at
the other people. All the guests were
dressed as fairy-tale characters! Giselle
touched her new, modern-looking
dress. This world was *so* confusing!

Then Giselle spotted Robert on the dance floor. He had come, too! He was dressed as a prince. He and his girlfriend, Nancy, walked up the stairs to greet them. Prince Edward asked Nancy to dance, leaving Robert and Giselle to dance with each other.

Robert and Giselle danced together beautifully. Giselle felt as if she were gliding on air. Then Nancy came over to take her dance partner back.

Giselle felt an unfamiliar feeling as she watched them dance. With a gasp, she realized what the feeling was—her heart was breaking!

Chapter 4

It was time to go back to Andalasia.
When Giselle told Prince Edward, he
hurried to get her coat. At that
moment, the old woman who had
pushed Giselle into the well appeared.
She held out a shiny apple.

"One bite, my love, and all this will go away." From up on the balcony, Giselle watched Robert and Nancy dance. Giselle felt her heart grow heavier still with sadness. She took a bite of the apple. Instantly, there was a clap of thunder. Giselle fell to the ground. Narissa had tricked her—again!

Prince Edward saw Giselle on the ground. "Someone help me! Please!" he called. Robert and Nancy ran to help. Robert spotted the apple. "She's been poisoned!" he shouted.

Dong! Dong! "When the clock strikes twelve, she'll be dead!" Narissa, who had turned back into her regular self, cackled.

No one knew how to save Giselle. As the clock continued to chime, Robert remembered what Giselle had said about the power of true love's kiss. "True love's kiss?" he suggested.

Prince Edward leaned over Giselle
and gently kissed her. He stood back
and waited for her to open her eyes.
But Giselle didn't move.

Dong! Dong! The clock chimed on.
Everyone looked at Robert. "It's not
possible. It couldn't be me!" he
exclaimed.

With only one stroke left until midnight, Robert kissed Giselle softly on the lips. "Please don't leave me," he whispered.

As the clock struck twelve, Narissa began to howl with delight. But then Giselle slowly opened her eyes. She looked right at Robert and smiled. "I knew it was you."

This was too much for Narissa. She grew so angry that she turned into a scaly beast. Grabbing Robert, she ran to the roof. Giselle raced after them with Prince Edward's sword in hand.

Narissa dangled Robert high above the street. "Put him down, Narissa!" Giselle demanded. Just then, Pip arrived. Together, the two friends battled the beast and won.

Soon after, Giselle and Robert were married. They started a dress company and made beautiful princess gowns for children. Nancy followed Prince Edward back to Andalasia and became the royal queen.

True love's kiss *was* the most powerful thing in the world. It had saved them all.